This book belongs to:

AVRORA

A B ♡

Retold by Monica Hughes
Illustrated by Priscilla Lamont

Reading consultants: Betty Root and Monica Hughes

This edition published by Parragon in 2009

Parragon
Queen Street House
4 Queen Street
Bath BA1 1HE, UK

ISBN 978-1-4075-8370-9

Printed in China

# The Princess and the Pea

PaRragon

Bath · New York · Singapore · Hong Kong · Cologne · Delhi · Melbourne

*Helping your child to read*

These books are closely linked to recognized learning strategies. Their vocabulary has been carefully selected from the word lists recommended by educational experts.

*Read the story*
Read the story
to your child
a few times.

The prince opened the door and there stood a girl.
"I am a princess," said the girl.
The girl was beautiful and wore a crown.
But she was very wet!
The prince liked the girl. But the queen said, "I will see if she is a real princess."

16

*Follow your finger*
Run your finger under
the text as you read.
Your child will soon begin to
follow the words with you.

*Look at the pictures*
Talk about the pictures. They will
help your child to understand the story.

"I am a princess." 17

*Give it a try*
Let your child
try reading the
large type on each
right-hand page.
It repeats a line
from the story.

*Join in*
When your child is ready, encourage
him or her to join in with the main
story text. Shared reading is the first
step to reading alone.

Once upon a time there was a lonely prince.
"You would not be lonely if you got married," said the queen.

But the prince didn't want to marry just anyone.
"I want to marry a princess," he said.

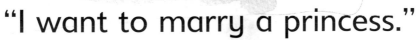

"I want to marry a princess."

The next day he went to look for
a princess.
He saw beautiful girls.
He saw girls who wore crowns.
But they were not real princesses.

He went to look for a princess.

The prince went back to see the queen.
He told her about the beautiful girls
and the girls who wore crowns.
He told the queen that they were not
real princesses.

The prince could not find a princess to
marry.
So he was still lonely.

The prince could not find
a princess.

That night there was a big storm.
There was thunder and lightning.
Then it rained and rained and rained.

In the middle of the night there was a
knock at the door.

There was a big storm.

15

The prince opened the door and there
stood a girl.
"I am a princess," said the girl.
The girl was beautiful and wore
a crown.
But she was very wet!
The prince liked the girl. But the
queen said, "I will see if she is a
real princess."

"I am a princess."

So the queen got some hard dried peas.
She made a bed for the princess.
The queen put a pea under the
mattress.
She put twenty mattresses on the bed.
She put twenty quilts on the bed.

The queen put a pea
under the mattress.

"This is your bed," the queen said to
the princess.
The princess had never seen a bed with
twenty mattresses and twenty quilts.
The princess climbed into bed.
"Good night," she said to the queen.

The princess climbed into bed.

But the princess could not sleep.
She was awake all night.

In the morning the queen came to see
the princess.
"Did you sleep well?" asked the queen.
"No, I was awake all night," said the
princess. "There was something hard in
the bed."

The princess could not sleep.

The queen went to see the prince.
"She is a real princess," said the
queen. "She felt the pea under twenty
mattresses and twenty quilts.
Only a real princess could do that."

"She is a real princess."

At last the prince had found a real
princess.
"Will you marry me?" he asked.
"Yes!" said the princess.
They were married the next day.
The prince was never lonely again and
they all lived happily ever after.

They were married
the next day.

# Look back in your book.
Can you read these words?

prince

peas

queen

mattress

princess

# Can you answer these questions?

Who came to the
door in the middle of
the storm?

What did the
queen put under
the mattress?

Who did the
prince marry?